I first met Mr. Mun at the end of October. I was searching for my springer spaniel, Ginger, who had gone missing the previous day. It was the first chilly day of fall, and as I walked down Pine Heights all the trees were bare branches scratching at the clouds. At the mouth of the alley that ran next to Mr. Mun's backyard, I noticed that his fence had three missing boards. What had once been a tight row of vertical slats, was now intersected by a gap large enough for my Ginger to crawl through. She was prone to sniffing around Mr. Mun's house because of Yoyo, his pug. Knowing about the bees, I walked low along his fence. A waft of burning cigarette drifted close as I approached the gap. I should have known then that he was near, but I was more concerned about being stung. I crept up to the fence and tilted my head forward to get a look into the yard, and a clump of my hair was grabbed in a tight fist. I was yanked through the gap in the fence. My shoulder and chest scraped against the small opening, and I was tossed onto a brick path in the middle of Mr. Mun's backyard.

He leaned over me, pinching my left hand between his thumb and index finger. I was immobilized with pain and fear that if either of us moved my hand would break. Mr. Mun, however, was not so worried. He kept me subdued with one hand and popped a cigarette into his mouth, straight out of its pack, with the other. He leaned in, rolling the unlit cigarette back and forth over his lips. "You tell me," he whispered, his accent reeking of nicotine. He tightened his two fingers, causing the pain in my hand to increase and further impair my ability to translate his broken English.

"Tell you what?" I begged.

"Why you break my fence?" His lips pursed as he leaned in, which caused his cigarette to flick down against his chin.

"My dog!" I screamed. His grip loosened. In hopes of distracting him from re-tightening, I gave him more information.

"I'm sorry, I thought Ginger might be in your yard. When I saw the hole in your fence..." He let go of my hand. The relief was so shocking that I forgot what I was saying. I felt like my entire body could float away.

Mr. Mun reminded me of the subject, "You looking for your dog?" He studied my eyes.

"Yes."

"So you did not break my fence and come in my yard?"

"NO WAY!" I shook my head to assist with potential translation problems. "I had nothing to do with this, Mr. Mun." Using his name seemed to help as well. He stood up, scanned the perimeter of his backyard, then leaned down and moved to grab my left hand again. I whimpered like a puppy who had just been hit by a bus, but he moved to my wrist and helped me to my feet.

"Sorry, Jasper."

"It's okay," I replied as I brushed mulch off my legs and rubbed my aching hand. The pain distracted me for a few seconds, until I realized where I was, Mr. Mun's backyard. The gardens around his yard glowed with colors that should have been reserved for spring or summer. I was mesmerized. Even in a wet and cold Baltimore fall, his backyard was vibrant.

"You see anybody around my house?"

When he asked me this question I realized what had most likely happened to his fence. Earlier today, when I was about to search for Ginger, I noticed Kevin Mooney, Donny Delatush and Joey Ives were congregating at the top of the alley. When I saw them I slowed down to let them get as far away as possible before I continued my search. Luckily, they were in a hurry and jumped over the guard rail that separated our houses from the daycare parking lot behind St. Agnes. I would not be surprised if they were the reason for the missing fence boards. Instead of sharing my theory with Mr. Mun, I stood enthralled with the beauty of his backyard. He slapped me across the cheek while holding me by the collar so I did not tumble across the stone pavers. My attention snapped back to him.

"Hey! I asked you a question," he said. "You on drugs or something?"

"No! I was just..." I stammered mesmerized by his flowers, the radiance whose only colorful competition in Violetville were the inflatable, holiday lawn decorations that litter so many yards. And even if there were no holiday near, there was always an inflatable Ravens linebacker or Oriole bird to keep on the lawn. "It's your yard," I mumbled through an aching cheek. Then I remembered what I should have been doing was looking for Ginger and not stopping to gush over Mr. Mun's flowers. I told him, "I was looking for my dog."

Mr. Mun let go of my collar. "You lose your dog?" He studied my face.

"Yes. Ginger disappeared yesterday." I looked at his fence and said, "I must have left my gate open." Even if I had left the gate open, my overweight, well-fed springer spaniel would have most likely just wandered to the front porch and taken a nap. Ginger knew exactly where her bread was buttered and never strayed too far. I looked around his yard, but Mr. Mun's pug dog, Yoyo, also seemed to be missing. She had the heart of a mastiff stuffed into a tiny pug and should have been rushing up to me defending her turf.

All the talk of missing dogs jogged my memory to Mark Warner. He and Kevin were always seen around the neighborhood with their own dog, a vicious collection of teeth and muscle named Warrior. A rude reality twisted my guts. For years Baltimore City police reports have spoken of local dog-fighting rings. The reports told of how dog fighting was rampant in the city, and whenever one venue was raided, another always popped up in some new row-home or project. My worries were the reports of how the criminals who run the rings steal other people's pets to use as practice for their fighting dogs. A practice that could not be good for any spaniel or pug. In the past year so many residents of Violetville and Morrell Park had lost their dogs that all the telephone poles in the neighborhood were covered with fliers. Neighbors offered rewards for any kind of information on the whereabouts of their missing companions. I thought, Those jerks dog-napped Yoyo, and most likely Ginger!

"Do you know those boys who were just in the alley?"

By default, his question promoted Mr. Mun to the new leader of my little one person search party. I was less afraid of Kevin and Mark if I believed Mr. Mun was on my side, and began to tell him everything I knew. "Yes, they are Kevin Mooney, Donny Delatush, and Joey Ives. Kevin lives across the street, next to Ms. Dinkels. But I'm not sure of the other guys..."

Mr. Mun put his hand up. He already knew where Kevin Mooney lived. "That's right." He looked down the street, and shifted his unlit cigarette. He was dealing with the realization

that one of his neighbors might have dog-napped Yoyo. Not

only that, but Kevin's father, Pat Mooney, had been one of the

fortunate recipients of free honey from Mr. Mun. The cost for a

jar of his honey was ten dollars, and Pat Mooney used his

welfare status to coerce Mr. Mun into giving it to him for free.

He claimed it cured his sleep apnea and gave him a new lease on

life. But, as Mr. Mun later told me, "being a big, fat jerk is why

Pat Mooney can't sleep."

Mark Warner was the d-facto, self-proclaimed leader of

Kevin, Donny, and Joey's gang. I'm not exactly sure where, but

Mark lived across Wilkens Avenue, somewhere near the train

tracks, on the outskirts of Violetville. He was the brazen type

who always presented himself with an air of recklessness that

made all of my neighbors not want to tussle with him. This was

before pit bulls were banned in Baltimore, and Mark used to

strut up and down Pine Heights with his dog, Warrior. The dog, a few steps ahead, carrying its leash in its mouth, daring anyone to complain with Mark always close behind, walking slowly, no matter how many cars accumulated on the single lane, one-way street. They would honk and yell, but this only made Mark laugh with his arms outstretched inviting any one of them to step out of their car and make him get out of the street. For all their fist shaking and honking, not one of them ever did anything.

Mark and Kevin once beat up one of their classmates, Rodney Kent, up near Benson Avenue. They were knocking his front teeth out with leather straps wrapped around their knuckles because they felt he shorted them on a bag of weed. Turns out they just didn't want to pay for the weed with money, but instead with a beating. Rodney screamed for help, and his grandma came running out with a broom in her hands and whacked Mark across the back of his head. Mark turned around and slapped her across the cheek. He dislocated her jaw, and she fell to the ground breaking both hips. He did 18 months at the

East Baltimore Juvenile Detention Center for that assault. (These were the quietest months in Violetville's recent history, ruined only by the fact that because of the length of his detention, Mark was now held back a few grades and would be in the same grade as me.) Rodney, however, unsure how his drug dealing element in the whole situation would pan out, didn't press any charges for his beating.

Everybody knew Mark and Kenny always had Warrior with them, but I never once thought they were involved in any dog fighting ring.

•

I stood outside the Mooney's house for about ten minutes, shifting on my feet as Mr. Mun pounded on their front door. I did not share Mr. Mun's fearless attitude. Mark and his gang of idiots were not much older than me. They had each failed several years of school, and when they actually showed up for classes it was usually just to let some poor sap know that they would be waiting for him after school. I was as worried about Kevin coming home and seeing me in his front yard, as I was about finding Ginger. I had heard of how these guys beat up people just for fun. How they didn't stop until they were bored, even if the victim was unconscious or sometimes even as the cops were pulling them off.

No one answered the door, so Mr. Mun stepped down from their stoop. We both headed back up the street and stopped in front of his house.

"Okay, Jasper, I have to fix my fence. Good luck with your dog."

I was not interested in sitting at home while Ginger was missing. I assumed she was with Mr. Mun's pug; and since Mr. Mun did not seem too worried about confronting the most apparent suspects in the dog-napping, I wanted to be near him when he did. I asked, "Mr. Mun, may I please help you fix the fence? Or maybe I could sweep your porch or something? I really don't want to go home right now."

Mr. Mun shifted his cigarette. He was not one to invite any neighbors into his backyard or house. In fact, not many of us had ever been on or in his property in my short lifetime. Meanwhile, his backyard was the one everybody wanted to see. It wasn't just his honey that made the entire neighborhood curious, but the stories that were told about the few glimpses of his backyard that different people had been able to witness over the years.

Only two houses had a direct view of Mr. Mun's backyard. One was Mr. Mun's next door neighbors, the Jonstons. But Mr. and Mrs. Jonston didn't talk too much about Mr. Mun's garden, and they did not entertain any of the rumors that circulated around the neighborhood, even the ones they started. The only other place with a direct view into Mr. Mun's backyard was from the windows of the top floor of Ms. Dinkels' house across the street.

Many years before I was born Mr. Mun moved into the long abandoned house on the opposite end of the same row of homes in which my father lived. My father was a carpenter and assumed Mr. Mun and he shared a passion for remodeling, since the unit he had purchased was in need of much repair. My father, the curious guy that he was, gave Mr. Mun less than a day to move in before he went down to greet him.

"Hello and welcome to the neighborhood. By the way, I'm a carpenter." My father always made it a point to let our neighbors know that he was available to help them with any project.

My dad claimed he met Mr. Mun at the gate to his backyard and that Mr. Mun was hesitant to allow him too far onto the property. However, dad eventually managed to talk his way into a tour of the yard and house. Everyone on Pine Heights was curious about this Korean fellow who had purchased the most dilapidated home on the block.

Dad recalled that on the second day of living on Pine Heights Mr. Mun was already well into landscaping his backyard. "There must'a been twenty of his buddies working all over that yard. Digging here, planting there. While others were filling in the holes with extra soil and covering everything with mulch. And still others were working on the pathways that were around the plots."

When Mr. Mun finished hustling my dad through all the upstairs floors he was put off when dad asked to have a look at the bottom floor. Dad was interested because most houses in Violetville that had finished basements only did so because of his hard work.

"Unfortunately, Mr. Fice, there is nothing to see down there."

"Oh, well, you know I'm a carpenter."

"Yes, you have mentioned that many times."

"Right." My dad looked around at all the silent workers going about their jobs. "I guess you got yourself covered in that department, don't you?"

"Yes, Mr. Fice. Thank you."

Mr. Mun's short-sentences and tone made it clear that the tour was over. Dad said, "Please call me, Gene."

"Yes, Gene," said Mr. Mun.

My dad, the cultural liaison that he was, attempted to explain his name for his new Korean neighbor, "That's short for Eugene."

"Yes, Eugene," Mr. Mun said, and gave my dad's hand a hurried shake. Of all our neighbors, my father is the only one who could claim to have been inside of Mr. Mun's house.

•

At some point after I was born, neighbors started wondering more and more about what was going on with Mr. Mun's garden. Originally, everyone had gotten their information from the Jonstons. They told my father that Mr. Mun had a lush garden of flowers that never died, and for nine months of the year the backyard buzzed with honey bees. The Jonstons mentioned how on any summer afternoon there would be so many bees in his garden that the vibrant colors of all the flowers were blurred by the flying black dots.

Mr. Jonston claimed that one morning he woke up and when he opened the blinds in his bedroom, he noticed Mr. Mun sitting cross legged in the middle of his garden. It was barely light out, but Mr. Jonston said, "I seen 'em. Them bees were swarming all over his head and shoulders. An' he's just setting there, still as a stone. It looked like they's gonna cover him up completely. So I turned around to rouse Cindy out of bed, and

17

when I turned back... he was nowhere to be seen. But those darn bees were still flying around, that's for sure."

The issue of the bees occupied the minutes of many a town hall meeting, as kids walking to school, and vagabonds and nurses cutting through the alley to get to St. Agnes, were stung on a regular basis. It appeared that anyone walking too close to the fence was going to be stung.

People were getting stung so often that they began to suspect it had something to do with the strange, end-unit row-house with the eight foot perimeter fence. However, it wasn't until Dontrel Cole was stung that the good folks of Violetville learned that Mr. Mun was actually raising the bees. (The Jonstons claimed that no hives were visible from their windows.) Dontrel was cutting through the alley after school and was dragging a stick across the planks of Mr. Mun's fence when he heard a buzzing noise and felt a searing pain in his left arm. He slapped the back of his arm and bolted home. By the time he was in his kitchen the bite had turned into a generous welt. The initial burning soon turned into a steady heat, and with each day Dontrel complained of a tight throbbing around his upper arm. So all the angry mothers and nurses banded together and sought my father's assistance. They assumed he was the best neighbor to approach Mr. Mun since he was the only neighbor to have ever talked with him at length. After hashing out the particulars of what and how my father was to approach Mr. Mun, the mob of neighbors moved out.

Mr. Mun met my father on his front porch. My neighbors waited on the sidewalk.

"Howdy, Mr. Mun." My dad squirmed a bit, as the energy from the mob was not really his style.

"Hello, Gene."

My dad didn't know how to begin the conversation. "Um, listen Mun..." Dad motioned over his shoulder towards the mob. "Our neighbors are concerned about the bee stings that their kids are getting when they get near your backyard. They're thinking that the bees are coming from your yard."

Mr. Mun interrupted him, "Oh no! I am sorry. Please wait just a minute." He left my dad standing on the porch. Meanwhile, dad turned around and raised his hands to let the people on the sidewalk know that he had everything under control. The screen door slammed shut and Mr. Mun was back with a large cardboard box in his arms. He put the box down and my dad saw the tops of small mason jars piled two jars high. Mr. Mun pulled out one of the jars and handed it to him.

"Please, Eugene, use this honey on the stings." Mr. Mun insisted that each neighbor take a jar of his homemade honey. "Please forgive me," he said, "My bees are very defensive of their garden. This honey will make the stings feel better."

As he handed out jars of honey, different neighbors thanked him, while others who couldn't understand his accent stood confused and staring at the jars in their hands. They wanted answers, not jars of honey with strange Korean symbols written on them.

"Wait just a minute, Mr. Mun," interjected Violetville's neighborhood know-it-all, Barbara Louise. Barbara really had no rightful place in the mob since she had never been stung, and had no children to be stung since it was determined that her husband was impotent. "We want to know what it is you're up to..." She held out the jar of honey in one hand while clenching the other in a fist and placing it, half-akimbo, on her hip.

Mr. Mun stopped and put on his most diplomatic face. "Ah yes. I know. Please understand that I am simply trying to raise bees to make honey. But most assuredly, this honey will soothe all the stings. Yes. Yes. And good remedy for other maladies as well." He finished by winking at Mrs. Louise.

The mob hushed. Mrs. Louise said, "How exactly can this honey help with maladies, Mr. Mun?"

Mr. Mun looked at her and said, "Well, for example, my honey can cure impotence."

Everyone knew Mrs. Louise's plight. She and her plumber husband Al had been trying for years to get pregnant and it never happened. Long ago they ran out of medical options, and Mrs. Louise grew more shrewish as it became clear that Al was the impotent one in the relationship. Meanwhile, her shrewishness drove Al to drink more and more alcohol. All of which exacerbated his beer belly, which exacerbated Mrs. Louise's disgust for him, and therefore, pushed them further apart.

Mr. Mun continued, "It will make your husband strong like tree trunk."

Mrs. Louise blushed a deep cheeky red and was about to say something when Mr. Mun interrupted. He leaned in close to Mrs. Louise and said, "It's okay. Tell him eat two tablespoons every day. You will have baby in no time."

Mrs. Louise's bottom lip trembled, "But... How...?"

Mr. Mun gently patted her shoulder. She stared at the jar in her hand, then turned and slumped home.

Mr. Mun passed out a jar of his homemade honey to each neighbor that mobbed his front yard, and they all left wondering how this peace offering solved the issue of the bees and their stinging. These questions were forgotten over the next several weeks.

After the dispersal of honey, things in Violetville started changing. Right away, when Mrs. Cole got home, she administered a glob of honey over the baseball sized welt on Dontrel's left arm. Within five minutes of the honey application the pain in his arm was gone, and fifteen minutes after that the welt was nothing more than an average insect bite. Mrs. Cole proceeded to eat three tablespoons.

Everyone who used the honey believed that it was a great boon for their lives. Mr. Perkins, up on Washington Street, claimed that when he rubbed it on his bald head hair started to grow back. All his neighbors agreed that they did indeed see little wisps poking their way through his scalp. Mrs. Williams, up on Coolidge, claimed that the honey rid her of her asthma and rid her seven year old son, Andy, of his "soupy lungs." My dad claimed that after eating a tablespoon every day his arthritis disappeared. "Not to mention I feel light on my feet," he told me. The veteran of the neighborhood, Colonel Jenkins claimed the honey rid him of his night-terrors. Mrs. Patrice gave it to her epileptic twin daughters, and they both have not had a seizure since.

Perhaps the most telling situation of all was when Barbara Louise's husband Al banged on Mr. Mun's door a little less than a week after Mr. Mun gave Barbara her first jar of honey. When Mr. Mun answered, he thought Al was there because he had learned of how Mr. Mun had told the neighborhood about his impotence. Al pushed the screen door out of the way and grabbed Mr. Mun around the shoulders, pulling him over the threshold. He wrapped his thick arms him and hugged him so tight that Mr. Mun could feel—despite Al having a rotund beer belly—the exact reason why Al was so grateful. He kissed Mr. Mun on the cheek and said, "You saved my life, Mun," and with that he broke out blubbering like a baby on Mr. Mun's porch. He continued, while sobbing, "You saved my marriage." He grabbed Mr. Mun's hands and squeezed, "My pipes are working again, man. Look!" He thrust his hips forward so Mr. Mun would have a clearer view of the erection that he'd had all morning. Mr. Mun backed away a few steps. Al wiped his tear-filled eyes, "Sorry man, I just can't thank you enough." Mr. Mun said it was okay and gave him another jar of honey. Within two months the Louises were pregnant with their first of what would be seven children.

Moms in Violetville began feeding tablespoons of the honey to their kids with each breakfast meal. Reports of bee stings in these kids disappeared. After several months, the only people being stung were the vagabonds and strangers who used the alley, anyone not fortunate enough to be a neighbor of Mr. Mun's.

As word spread, neighbors who weren't involved in the mob came knocking on Mr. Mun's door. Eventually, the entire neighborhood was lining up so often to receive a jar of Mr. Mun's miracle honey that he called a town-hall meeting at Violetville Elementary School. It was a record meeting in that a representative from every household in Violetville, except Ms. Dinkels', was present.

"Okay," Mr. Mun raised a hand. "Please, in regards to my honey, it is very important that we keep its beneficial qualities within the borders of Violetville."

The neighbors shifted a bit in their seats. Not all of them understood his accent, but all were relieved when they realized that Mr. Mun was not ending their honey supply. In fact, they didn't care when Mr. Mun told them that, due to the high demand, he was going to start charging ten dollars for each jar of honey. He could have charged one hundred dollars and every neighbor in Violetville would have found the money. He finished the meeting by saying that the return of a previous jar would get anyone a dollar off their next purchase of honey. "But please, let us all agree that this honey is our little secret. Something to keep all of us in Violetville happy and healthy."

The entire standing-room-only crowd understood Mr. Mun's last request and answered in unison, "YES, PLEASE!"

"So, may I please hang out down here with you? I want to help find our dogs."

Mr. Mun couldn't refuse my pleas. His usual matter-of-fact demeanor gave way to a softer face that finally broke as he said, "Okay, Jasper, you can help."

We walked through his front door and into a sparsely lit living room with low sofas against two walls. At the ends of each sofa sat small, ornate tables with tasseled lampshades on which were strange Korean symbols. The coffee table in the middle of the room was also long and ornate, and draped down the middle was a golden, fringed runner with lotus silhouettes printed on it. On this runner sat a silver tray with candles melted to different lengths. The far end of the table was a few feet in front of a gas stove that sat in what used to be a fireplace. Above the mantle hung a sword that also had fine carvings in the scabbard. Resting on a small stand on the mantle was a long tube wrapped in tight, black cloth, which displayed a ceremonial design. The wall space was decorated with Korean calligraphy drawings and silk prints centered between the corners and windows. The furniture was out of place, and the smell reminded me of sugar. Nothing about this room spoke of what I knew of Baltimore.

"Jasper, move your ass!" Mr. Mun hurried me through the kitchen, which looked more like a typical Baltimore room with few signs of anything Korean, besides the rice steamer, then out the back door. I stood on the porch and for the second time today was in the presence of the vivid colors of his garden.

"You stay here. I will get the tools." As he walked toward his shed, he turned and said, "Keep watch on the Mooney's house. I will be right back."

From his back porch, I had a clear view of all the houses down the southern half of Pine Heights. The Mooney's house was easy to see.

I heard a few clanks and thunks before Mr. Mun appeared from his shed with a small, black tool bag in one hand, and in the other was a long beam of cedar.

"What the heck is that?"

"My replacement for the broken fence."

"Yeah, but that's a four by four."

Mr. Mun handed the cedar beam over to me. Because I was standing on his porch, the top of the beam was shoulder height. I let it rest on my shoulder while Mr. Mun made another trip to the shed, and after a few loud scrapes he dragged a portable table-saw out onto his pathway.

"I know what it is Jasper."

Then it dawned on me that Mr. Mun was going to mill his own fence planks. His fence was a long row of planks set tightly together, and which were nailed to two runners that spanned the eight foot space between the posts. The planks were square at the top and bottom, and the top was finished with a long horizontal piece. A simple, sturdy and elegant style that blocked all view through the fence, and could be easily repaired, even by the teenage son of a carpenter.

"By the way, Mr. Mun," I explained. "I've been helping my dad for the past few summers."

Mr. Mun stopped moving the table-saw. He looked up at me. "Jasper, you know how to work a table-saw?"

"Of course. I'm the cut guy for my dad when I help him."

Mr. Mun walked up on the porch and said, "You are now cut guy in my backyard."

I was on the brink of achieving something that my father had long dreamed about, helping Mr. Mun. I hurried down the steps to the saw.

"Okay, you rip this plank all the way." He motioned up and down the 4 x 4 with an open hand. "Then cut each one to length."

This was an easy task for me. By the first rip, Mr. Mun could see I was comfortable around his table-saw. He went back up on the porch and stood on the top step so he could oversee his carpentry job while keeping an eye on the Mooney's house. I had the three planks ripped in no time. "Do you want me to sand them?"

"No. Keep it rough. Now grab my hand saw and cut the planks down to 108 inches."

"You sure? Do you want me to measure..."

"NO! Just do as I say."

"Okay." I answered. Mr. Mun was strict, and his quick flashes of instructions made me anxious. I was not used to this, as my father was always patient and understood that I was still a novice carpenter. I measured the planks and cut them to length with Mr. Mun's pull saw.

"Good. Now take my hammer and those nails and from the other side of fence, nail the planks to the cross pieces. You understand, Jasper?"

"Yes sir."

I was impressed that Mr. Mun was having me use these hand tools, as whenever I worked with my father we always used power tools or pneumatic nailers. This, however, was an easy job, too small to require setting up the air compressor and the nail guns. In just a few minutes I knocked the last nail into the third plank. Placing the hammer at my feet, I collected the box of nails and my steel tape. All my tools secured, I reached for the hammer when a foot came out from behind me and stepped on the back of my hand. I thought it was Mr. Mun coming to tell me that I had not properly fixed the fence, but the style of shoe spoke of a younger, American foot. It turned out to be Kevin Mooney. He was cutting through the alley on his way home when he saw me from the daycare parking lot and snuck up on me like an alley cat on an unsuspecting mouse. My hand hadn't quite recovered from Mr. Mun's earlier pinching, so when Kevin ground his heal into it I felt like my wrist would surely break.

"Owww, Kevin!" I made it a point to yell his name in hopes that Mr. Mun might hear.

"What are you doing, Jasper?" Kevin removed his foot from my hand and delivered a fist to my nose. I fell onto a puddle of my own blood. I looked up at my assailant and gave him a kick to the side of his shin. It only made him angrier.

"Don't you kick me, you little..." He pounded an agonizing kick into my low-back, and then bent down and grabbed me by my chin, forcing me to look up at him. "Why are you working on this fence, Jasper?"

I realized that Kevin had no idea Mr. Mun and I were on to his dog-napping scheme. He was just pissed that someone whose ass he could kick was fixing his vandalism. Any defensive attempt was better than none, so I swung my foot again and choked out a mumbled, "Fuck you, Kevin. Where's my dog?"

His grip on my face tightened. "What did you just say?"

I spoke low in hopes of stalling for time. "I can't answer you when you're holding my jaw like this."

He let go and my body sank back onto my elbow. I pinched the top of my nose, right between the eyes to stave off the steady flow of blood, and repeated, "Where's my dog?" Kevin cocked his right hand into the air. I braced. His fist moved up into the direction of the sun, blocking its glare from my eyes, and in the shadow of Kevin Mooney's fist, in the half-second before it was to fall down upon my face, a cedar 4 x 4 swung out of my peripheral vision and smashed into Kevin's forearm. Kevin screamed and jumped back. Mr. Mun knelt down next to me while Kevin began his tirade.

"YOU FUCKING CHINK! YOU BROKE MY FUCKING ARM!" His voice was high-pitched and terrified.

35

Though there was fear in his voice, I found it relieving to see Kevin dancing around the alley with his left hand clenched above his right elbow, as if letting go would mean the forearm might fall off. Tears poured out of his face as he cursed at Mr. Mun and me.

Mr. Mun looked at my face. I didn't like his expression when he saw all the blood. He said nothing, then stood up to address the issue of Yoyo with Kevin. In that short time, however, Kevin had made his way down the alley, over the guard rail and was half-way across the daycare parking lot. Mr. Mun did not pursue. He scored big, and he knew Kevin had to return home sooner or later. He looked down at me. "You look like shit." He pulled me to my feet, saying, "We'll get ice. Don't forget my tools, Jasper," and walked off with the cedar beam over his shoulder.

•

In Mr. Mun's kitchen he insisted that I sit down at the breakfast table. I sat down and Mr. Mun came over with a jar of honey and a spoon. He scooped up a glob of honey and smeared it across the swollen side of my face, as well as my nose. By that time I was unable to breathe out of my nose, so all the honey that he packed into my nostrils didn't affect me.

"This will help relieve the pain and swelling." He wrapped a mound of ice in a dishtowel and pressed it into the glob of honey on the side of my face, then moved my hands to hold it. When I opened my good eye he had disappeared down the steps and left the door wide open. It creaked closed a few inches. Since I couldn't hear any activity from Mr. Mun in the basement, I leaned forward a few inches to see if I could get a glimpse of anything down there, but I was not able to see much more than the first few steps.

I moved enough to see the white glow of florescent lights that hung from drop-ceiling panels. The little bit of floor I could see was spotless, and off to the side of the steps was the corner of a clean white table. I decided that it was safe to get a closer look and stood up from my chair. With the cold compress still pressed to my face, I moved across the kitchen. Standing to one side of the basement door, I listened. My swollen nose felt warm, but the deep ache had disappeared.

There was no sound coming from the basement. While listening, I moved the cold compress to the other side of my face and saw a drop of blood splat on the threshold of the door. I knelt down and tried to wipe it up, but I used the bloody towel that had been wrapped around my compress, and instead of cleaning anything, I just smeared a bloody streak across Mr. Mun's linoleum. Then, I heard a door open in the basement, which was followed by a low humming. Mr. Mun mumbled something and closed the door. The humming ceased. This hastened my cleaning attempts, but Mr. Mun was up the steps and looming over me before I could stand up. Our eyes locked. In one hand he held a bottle of liquor, and in the other was a jar of honey.

"Jasper," he asked, "What are you doing?"

I tightened up, and stood up straight as if I'd been caught cheating on a test. I had no idea what to say. I tried, "I'm sorry. I didn't see anything. I was just curious. Please don't be angry..."

He glared and gave his current unlit cigarette several tosses back and forth in his mouth. "Sit down."

Mr. Mun brought two highball glasses filled with ice cubes to the table. He scooped a mound of honey into both glasses before pouring an equal amount of the liquor over the honey and ice cubes. He pushed one across the table.

I put my hands up. "Um, I am not 21?"

He stared at me, as if he couldn't understand why my age mattered, shrugged, and placed both glasses in front of him. He said, "Too bad for you then," and sipped from his glass. His eyes closed as he relaxed and drew a deep breath. A sour whiskey smell wafted across the table. It reminded me of how my dad smelled at Thanksgiving and Christmas dinner.

Mr. Mun settled deeper into his chair. As he relaxed, I realized that he didn't really care that he had just caught me snooping. Though, when he said, "I suppose, Jasper, you saw my lab," my face heated up. I was embarrassed and a bit scared. Mr. Mun looked up at the ceiling. His eyes, however, were off somewhere else much farther away. "And I guess you heard the buzzing?"

"Yes, sir. I did hear the buzzing."

He sipped.

"But...is that a problem? I mean, I don't think anybody cares how you raise your bees, Mr. Mun."

"I do, Jasper." He sipped again. "It is not the people in this neighborhood that I worry about."

"Well, I'm not saying a word to anybody. I promise," We both sat back, he sipped and I switched the ice pack to the other side of my face. The energy between us seemed to be relaxing. I asked, "So, are you a scientist?"

Mr. Mun sneered and mumbled something in Korean, before scooping another mound of honey into a freshly iced glass and topping it with the liquor. He answered, "I am a bio-chemist." He took a long draught from his glass, and continued, "The tables you saw and bees you heard are the remainder of my life's work."

"Your life's work?"

"My studies at University were in bio-chemistry, with an emphasis on stinging and biting insects. I loved spiders and scorpions, but most of all, bees. My scores were top of my class, so naturally I was hired by the State. Before I fled Korea I was doing research in the government's chemical warfare division. I advanced quickly, which consequently allowed me to learn things that I was not comfortable knowing. Such as, what my work was contributing to… I should have known better, Jasper. I was lucky to have had a job in the first place with a nice house and enough food for my… family." His eyes returned to the ceiling, and he sipped. "I had no other employment options besides working in the chemical division" He looked again at the ceiling, and took another sip. "I just wanted to work with bees, Jasper. I believe in everything that the bees can do." He looked up, as if the ceiling wasn't there, and after a heavy sigh said, "My government just wanted different things."

His nostalgic demeanor turned to a scowl. He continued, "I tried to compromise, and when it was discovered that I had asked for a transfer to another laboratory, my security clearance was revoked. Before I got home that night, my family was gone. I knew then that I needed to move farther away than my parents' farm in Paekam."

Shaking the cubes in his glass, he continued, "I had friends Jasper, but they couldn't risk their own families. When you leave Korea, you leave your soul behind." He slurred and his accent grew. "But the US made it easy for me to get out. Mostly, they wanted to know if I had anything to do with my country's nuclear program, which I did not. I told them everything, and they gave me amnesty."

I wasn't sure at this point if his stare was the liquor or him chasing some long lost memory. He continued, "I was the golden boy for something like three months. They listened to everything and anything. I gave up all of my experience with no problem." He sipped and looked back at my swollen face. "Jasper, I did not support my country's decisions or intentions. There was nothing good that could come from what they wanted me to do. But I miss the mountains of my homeland." He drank the last mouthful of liquor and slapped the glass on the table.

I sat frozen. My short Baltimore life had given me no way to fathom what Mr. Mun's life might have been like in Korea. I was grateful he allowed me to hear his story. Shifting the cold compress on my face, I said, "Mr. Mun. I'm sorry things ended up like this." I tried changing the subject, "So, why do you keep the bees in the basement?"

He looked at me from behind a fresh, unlit cigarette. "It is safer for everybody that way, Jasper."

"Oh."

"Most days of the year the bees come and go through a tube in my basement window, and they never stray too far from my backyard. I have planted all the flowers they need. In return they give me an endless supply of honey." He could see I was still confused. "If I kept them outside, Jasper, they would die in the winter. My system allows me more control of their swarming."

I knew what a swarm was, and I did not want to meet up

with a swarm of Mr. Mun's bees.

"Jasper, would you like to see?"

•

He stood on the landing, yanking a pull-chain for the overhead light before motioning for me to follow him down the steps. The lights in the basement glowed a stark white fluorescent tone. I reached the last step and felt as awestruck as when I had witnessed Mr. Mun's backyard. The basement was divided into three different rooms. All the walls were painted a high-gloss white, increasing the reflection of the overhead light. Everything was clean, and there was no musty odor.

The stairs split the floor down the middle, and in the section to my right were four, 6' fold-out tables. Each table was occupied with chemistry lab equipment. Glass beakers full of colorful, bubbling liquids sat atop bunsen burners that filled the room with a gentle hissing sound. At the end of one table sat a centrifuge similar to the one I had used in my chemistry class. Behind the tables, and lining the entire side wall, was a shelf unit packed with everything from boxes of lab equipment, normal household goods, and stacks of Korean cigarettes.

The overhead fluorescents paled in comparison to the glow that emanated from a window at the far end of the basement. This window encompassed the majority of a wall that stretched across the width of the room. Mesmerized, I stood an inch from the glass. I had to squint. Mr. Mun shoved a pair of protective goggles in my hand. My eyes acclimated to the goggles' tint and the colors of the room in front of me were not diminished. Hanging from the ceiling were many different types of lighting, below which grew a vibrant indoor garden with more plant and flower species than most people in Violetville grew in their yards.

Mr. Mun stood next to me. "This is my propagation room."

"Propagation room?"

"Yes. Every flower in this room produces a different result."

"What do you mean?"

47

"Through the synthesis of the bees honey-making, all the benefits of the different flowers are combined into a tonic that is more healing then any antibiotic produced in a lab. By growing certain flowers, I can control the properties of the honey. In addition to that, I can increase certain elements of the honey to improve potency. My bees are natural chemists, Jasper." He smiled, but I wasn't sure if it was because of pride in his bees or because he knew he was making me nervous.

His honey had incredible healing capabilities, but I was beginning to sense that Mr. Mun didn't just make honey. I asked, "So, what are all these flowers? Why are they in PVC pipes?"

"This is a soil-less system." He continued, "Those pink flowers are Hawthorn, which is good for your cardiovascular system. Those yellow and orange ones are Calendula, which is good for helping your body heal. Those over there are Echinacea, which also helps your immune system."

I was buzzing with questions and tried to remember all the names that he described. At the back of the propagation room, behind the tables of flowers, were a few tree-like plants and shrubs that grew out of their own soil filled pots. I asked, "Why are those plants growing in their own pots? They look like small trees."

"Yes, Jasper, those are trees that I have trimmed to thrive in my basement."

"Oh, you mean like a big bonsai tree?"

Mr. Mun sighed and said, "Yes, Jasper, like a bonsai."

"What kind of tree is the one with the white flowers?"

He paused for a few seconds and said, "That is Nux Vomica.'

"What does it do?"

Mr. Mun turned back to the glass and chewed on his unlit cigarette. "Let's just say, it helps rid you of infection."

I tried to keep up with all that Mr. Mun was showing me. Just the name, Nux Vomica, made me a bit squeamish. I was about to probe further with more questions about the plant when Mr. Mun pointed to the small section of wall to the left of the window. Protruding about 4" out of this wall was a 6" PVC pipe, with a cap on its end.

"That is how the bees access this room."

"Where do the bees come from?" I remembered hearing a buzzing noise when I was in the kitchen but had seen no bees down here.

"This room here," he answered and pointed across the basement to a wall on the other side of the stairs. Unlike the propagation room, in the far wall was an oddly placed small window at about my eye height next to the door from which I had earlier seen Mr. Mun emerge. The scene in the room was lit by a single window that was right below the ceiling. Mr. Mun flicked a light switch and the room was washed in a dull red glow. Protruding from the window was a capped PVC pipe over which crawled a dark mass of bees. This was their exit to the backyard garden. On the floor sat stacks of wooden hive boxes. The entrances to the different hives were busy with the same black dots that covered the PVC pipe. I leaned towards the glass and looked to my right at the wall that was shared with the grow room. There was the other end of the PVC pipe that led to the hydroponic room. It spanned the lab and died into the propagation room wall.

I asked, "Why are their exits closed now?"

"My bees are in flux, Jasper. You see that?" He pointed down towards the hive-room's floor. Scattered about the floor were piles of dead bees.

"My colonies are in a cull. That pile you see on the floor are all the dead."

"Why are the bees fighting?"

"Not fighting. Preparing. It's that time of year when they need to get ready for the colder months. When all they have is the inside garden. They are well aware of how much honey they have in relation to their population. By the looks of that pile, I would say they have less honey than can sustain them." He shook his head. "I have been too generous with the honey, and now there is not enough to feed the bees that make it."

"How do they know who dies and who lives?"

He looked at me, "This is Darwinism at its best, Jasper. What you see is every bee for himself. A fight to the death. The queen orders the cull to begin, and then she stops it when the population's balance has been restored. After the cull, any bee still alive gets to live another season."

He smiled and touched his fingers to the window. His face got as close as the end of his unlit cigarette. He continued, "It is amazing."

"Why?"

"Because they fight to kill, but in so doing, their stingers become stuck in their opponent and they end up dying too. Yet if they do survive, when the cull is over, they go right back to business as usual feeding the larva and making more honey. After all this, the bees that live through the cull really don't live too long into the next season. It does not make sense to humans, yet this process is the nature of the bees." He looked back in the hive room and sighed.

As I processed all of what he told me, I tried to keep the conversation going. Pointing to the large mass of bees crowding the exit tube, I asked, "Why do you close off their exit?"

"I do not want them to leave until the cull is over. Otherwise they would swarm and I would most likely lose them. Not to mention, in this type of frenzy, the neighborly repercussions would be a big problem. This is how those assholes were able to take Yoyo."

"What do you mean?"

He looked at me again, this time more intent. "My bees would not have let them get away with what they did. You see, Jasper. These bees do not like disharmony. This neighborhood is as much theirs as it is ours, including those hoodlums. Any aggressive movements or energies and the bees will protect their colony. You have been stung by these bees before. I'm sure you are aware of how a swarm would easily change a dog-thief's mind." He smiled again, "Remember, Jasper a community is a living thing. It too can become infected."

His eyes went back in the hive room. After a deep inhale he said, "We could learn a lot from honey bees." As he continued, a low buzzing was heard and a solitary bee bounced on the window and buzzed past Mr. Mun's face. We both watched it fly around the room. Mr. Mun walked over to the lab table with the lit bunsen burner on it.

"Not just in the test tubes, Jasper." He leaned over and in the bunsen burner lit the cigarette that had been in his mouth all morning. "They are very pragmatic. Life for the bees is black and white," he said while following the lone bee around the lab. He puffed a plume of cigarette smoke in front of the air borne bee. It landed on his shoulder. He looked at me. "Everyone understands their place, does their job, and works towards survival of the species." He walked over to the door and took a long drag on his cigarette. The door sucked air as he opened it. He blocked as much of the opening with his leg and ribs, as if to prevent any bees from leaving the hive room. He exhaled a huge cloud in front of the few inches of opening that remained and angled his shoulder with the bee into it. It lifted off and found its place back amongst the hive and the cull. Mr. Mun looked back at me. "And no one tries to change the rules."

•

We watched through the window for a few more minutes. I was digesting all that was just discussed when a loud metallic noise, like someone kicking the screen door, startled us. Mr. Mun and I hurried up the steps. When I reached the kitchen, he was pulling the front door open. He stood staring out into the yard. I could not see onto the porch or in the yard, but I heard him gasp. He growled Korean curses. I strained to get a glimpse of what was blocking the screen door, and I saw that it was the carcass of Yoyo. Her head was contorted in a gross, unnatural fashion. Her blank eyes were opened and stared up as if accusing her beloved owner of not keeping a close enough watch over her. She had been used as practice for Mark Warner's pit bull, Warrior; a small, defenseless dog, used more for keeping the taste of blood fresh in a killer's mouth than for any sort of martial challenge.

Mr. Mun picked her up and turned to me, saying, "Jasper, take Yoyo to the kitchen." He flicked his cigarette butt into the sand-filled ashtray that sat next to his front door before moving to the top step of his porch.

From the sidewalk in front of Mr. Mun's house Donny Delatush yelled, "That's right you chink, motherfucker." He was flanked by Jim Ives and a bleary-eyed Kevin Mooney. In the few hours that Mr. Mun and I had been talking in his kitchen and staring at his bee hives, Kevin had acquired a splint for his right arm. It was stained with blood and looked like the local Boyscout troop had used his arm for first aid drills. He also looked like he might be on lots of pain killers. Donny and Joey did all the talking.

Worse than the sight of the three of them, was that they were accompanied by Warrior. He was on a leash held by Joey. And at first, he seemed only interested in sniffing the sidewalk and grass, but even this normal dog behavior challenged Joey to keep the pit-bull close. Soon his grip on the leash, in addition to the tense energy he was creating with his verbal assaults, snapped Warrior's head up from his sniffing. Warrior moved to face Mr. Mun's house and began to bark towards the porch. He wasn't the type of dog to leap and jump while tethered, but he was aware that the person on the other end of the leash was not his trainer, which meant limits could be pushed. He growled at Mr. Mun and pulled Joey, inch by inch, into the yard.

Mr. Mun held the broom that he used every morning to sweep his porch. He moved it so it leaned against the newel post, saying, "I suggest you people leave."

"Oh you want us to 'reave' your yard..." Joey and Donny laughed as they mocked his accent. As they yelled, Warrior tensed and pulled. His anger was fueled by the hatred in his handlers' words. Whenever Joey regained his footing, the dog leaned further into the leash and dug his paws deeper into the grass. But Joey's energy was turbulent and soon Warrior couldn't help but become a snarling mass of torqued muscles. He jumped forward again, pulling the leash from Joey's hand.

"Warrior! NO!" Joey yelled, most likely more worried about the damage Mark would do to him if anything happened to his champion fighting dog than about any damage Warrior might do to another person.

Warrior sprang towards the steps. In the second it took Warrior to leap, Mr. Mun stepped back on his left foot and raised his right. I thought he was getting into a defensive posture, but his foot dropped onto the broom handle that leaned on his porch post. The handle snapped in half, rending two pieces with splintered ends. The force of his kick caused the top piece to flip down into his right palm that was already waiting to catch it.

Warrior continued forward, and in less than a second was more than half-way down Mr. Mun's walkway. One more second and he leapt again, clearing all four of the front steps. He was flying through the air ready to sink his teeth into anything in front of him. In that short second, Mr. Mun pivoted back on his left heel a full 360 degrees. Then, he used the momentum of his pivot and stepped towards the oncoming pit-bull, slamming the splintered end of the broom handle into Warrior's ribcage. The dog yelped a quick screech, wriggled on the stick a few times before coughing a bloody spray off his tongue as his body deflated.

Mr. Mun looked up, and using the broken broom handle, lifted Warrior's body into the air. He held the dog above his head for the few seconds it took to shift the unlit cigarette out of the path of dog blood that splashed down the right side of his face. Warrior squirmed and hissed a few wet whimpers leading into a louder, hollow rasp as he was tossed back to the feet of his handlers. Mr. Mun still held the piece of broom handle. Blood soaked the splinters and ran down over his knuckles. Warrior thumped and rolled, lifeless, across the lawn. Kevin was no longer drowsy. He pushed Joey out of the way with his good left hand

and stood above Warrior. "Mother fucker," he said, and looked up at Mr. Mun. Donny and Joey inched their way towards the alley.

Mr. Mun moved down one step towards Kevin and whispered, "Take a step closer Kevin. Please step onto my yard." Their eyes locked while my heart raced.

Kevin abandoned the staring contest first and yelled, "Joey, we can't leave Warrior here." Joey ran over and dragged Warrior's body from Mr. Mun's property before picking him up and hurrying around the corner to catch up with Donny who had already jumped the guard-rail. Kevin turned to look at Mr. Mun. He was breathing heavy and for a few seconds had to hold on to the corner of Mr. Mun's fence. He took a huge inhale and stood up. His eyes scanned Mr. Mun's property and wandered up the street for a second, like he had forgotten what he was doing. Soon he regained focus and turned back toward us. Supporting himself on the fence, he pointed at Mr. Mun and said, "This aint over."

•

The cops did not take long to arrive. With the evidence that lay in Mr. Mun's kitchen, they scribbled on their pads and made a lot of claims that they would "get right on it". They asked that my father come down while they questioned me. When he arrived we settled in at the kitchen table, and one of the police officers pulled a chair up and sat between us.

"Okay son, you say you did not see the boys kill the pug. Correct?"

"Yes."

"And you claim that these same kids took your dog? A springer spaniel?" The officer scribbled.

"I do think they took my dog. Yes." Dad was learning for the first time the most likely fate of Ginger.

"And, you claim they hang out with Mark Warner?" The officer was already familiar with the name, like most cops at the local station.

"Yes." I repeated the other three names and reminded him that Kevin lived just a few doors down the street.

Soon my questioning ended and I was ushered home by the police. I skulked up the block not wanting to be far from the action. Plus, I was pretty shaken up and my head was swimming with all the information Mr. Mun had shared. Dad stuck around Mr. Mun's to keep his nose close to the situation. As usual, the police said they'd handle everything, and made it a point to let my dad know that cases like these are very difficult to solve.

"There are a lot of dog-fighting rings in this city," explained the same officer that questioned me. "It's tough to bust one up for just one dog, but your son gave us some pretty good leads to start with."

"Thank you sir," replied my dad. When he returned home, the usual evening events happened and nothing much was discussed. Dinner was eaten. The dishes were cleaned. Television was watched, and I went up to my room. Sleep, however, was hard to come by. The pain in my face, the awful death of Yoyo, and my missing Ginger compelled me to toss and turn on top of my sheets for hours. Meanwhile, the moon moved behind the street light that stood at the front of the alley next to our end of the row. It is because of this streetlight that I am not sure when I last slept in darkness. By the time the moon was about to disappear behind my window frame, from down the street, I heard glass being smashed. I bolted up and flung my window open. Again, in front of Mr. Mun's house were the troublemakers, Kevin, Donny and Joey, only this time they were joined by Mark Warner. He stood in the front of the group and waited as Joey placed something in his hand. Mark looked down at the object, and then at Mr. Mun's house as he yelled, "Hey CHINK!" He tossed the object at the house and another window shattered. "I need to talk to you."

Donny and Joey were busy behind him picking up more rocks and supporting him with an occasional slander. Rocks thumped against the bricks and smashed as much glass as possible. Despite their vehemence, the gang made it a point to be as quiet as possible so as to only attract attention from their victim, but from my end of the row, I could tell the nature and the volume of their threats were escalating. I looked up and down Pine Heights to see if any neighbor might be coming to Mr. Mun's aid. The street was empty, and houselights began to turn off. I gave my neighbors the benefit of the doubt and assumed that, like me, they were too afraid of Mark Warner and hoped they were calling the cops from the safety of their home phones. Even Mr. Mooney, Kevin's father, didn't seem to care. Not one light came on in his run-down house across the street. I was pretty sure he was about to lose his free honey supply.

As I was watching the vandalism ensue, I was impressed to see that, in fact, one of my neighbors was coming to Mr. Mun's assistance. The ruckus these four were making had awoken Ms. Dinkels. From behind her azaleas, she jumped, hissed and clawed at the air between her and the vandals. Her bravery, despite being born of craziness, filled me with admiration and adrenaline. Donny, however, also noticed Ms. Dinkels and motioned Joey to go over and shut her up. They both laughed as Joey walked across the street yelling, "Shut the fuck up you old bat!"

Ms. Dinkels jumped and hissed. As Joey got closer, her activity became more frenzied, and she started running back and forth, behind the azaleas, from corner to corner of her front yard. I was impressed, but worried that Joey was about to hurt another innocent neighbor. As I watched him walking across the street, the darkness played tricks on my eyes. I thought I saw a quick silhouette dash between a few cars across the street then disappear into the darkness behind Ms. Dinkels' house. None of the troublemakers saw the strange form.

My attention was drawn back to the ruckus. The Jonstons' porch light blinked on. Mark startled and threw the stone in his

hand at their house front. Another smash of glass and the light
went dark.

I decided I would try to distract the hoodlums until the cops
showed up. If nothing else, I hoped to lure Joey away from Ms.
Dinkels in order to give Mr. Mun a better chance of defending
his property. I choked back a large gulp of fear, and was about to
hustle to my front door when I noticed Joey stopped in the
middle of the street. He let out a quick, "Ow! What the..," and
slapped at something on the side of his neck. He jerked his
shoulders around 360 degrees, as if to defend himself against
some unseen attack. Nothing was there, so he walked back to his
gang checking over both shoulders and pressing his hand into
his neck. Ms. Dinkels was left alone.

Meanwhile, on his way down the walk-way towards Mr.
Mun's porch, Mark came to an abrupt halt and slapped his hand
against the back of his neck. "Mother Fucker," he yelled jumping
a quick 180 degrees, as if he might catch a glimpse of whatever

had just bitten him. He stood on the walk-way with his hand on the back of his neck and searched down towards his feet.

I froze and watched as Donny, too, let out a small, "Hey!" and jumped to his right. By this point, Joey was making his way towards the alley while Donny cursed and switched arms as he tried to reach something between his shoulder-blades. One moment his arms flailed over his head, and the next they were contorted behind his back as he tried to grab something just out of reach.

Then came Kevin's turn. He snapped out of his daze and slapped at something on his right shoulder. He, however, was able to reach whatever it was, and pinched it between his fingers. He waved to Mark, who was still scanning the ground and walked over to him. They stared at whatever was in Kevin's hand. Donny came over to look. The three of them then shook their heads and moved nervously on their feet. Finally, Kevin dropped whatever he held and they all hurried out of view. This time Kevin did not follow them down the alley. He walked

home, pausing once to brace himself on the hood of a

neighbor's car. Each step seemed to be getting weaker. I watched

as he disappeared into the darkness that surrounded his home,

and right before I looked away I noticed, again, a silhouette

running back across the street. As it ducked behind a car and

then ran into the alleyway, I noticed what looked like a long pole

or tube in the person's hand.

The mayhem had lasted only ten minutes and then ended as

quickly as it started. I watched and waited in eager silence for

whatever might happen next, and I soon noticed Mr. Mun

standing on his front lawn at the distance that the gang had been

standing when they were smashing his windows. He looked up

and down the street and then bent down to pick something off

the ground. His hand moved to his pocket. When he stood back

up, I noticed that there was a lit cigarette in his right hand. He took a long drag, exhaled a cloud over his head, smashed the butt into the sole of his slipper, and went back inside.

The police arrived at Mr. Mun's house for their second visit in less than 24 hours. This time, there were about seven squad cars, and the lights and noise from the officers was more disturbing than the previous hoodlums' antics. They taped off Mr. Mun's yard and milled about in the glow of their cruisers' lights. The officer interviewing Mr. Mun was one of our neighbors, Officer Wayne. He too was an avid consumer of Mr. Mun's honey, claiming that it brought much relief to his boggy prostate.

While conversing on his sidewalk, Mr. Mun and Officer Wayne looked from each other towards the Mooney's house. After about an hour, Officer Wayne was the only cop remaining. Mr. Mun went inside, then returned with a jar of honey, and passed it over to Officer Wayne. He took the gift and put it in the trunk of his cruiser before walking back to Mr. Mun to shake his hand as they parted ways. Throughout the night, not one of the police

officers stopped at the Mooney's house.

•

The next morning I awoke to the sounds of more sirens on Pine Heights. Down the street was an ambulance parked in front of the Mooney's house. A few small groups of neighbors stood around and talked, while the EMTs hurried about.

Mr. Mooney had woken up to find Kevin dead on their living room floor. The coroner who performed his autopsy commented on how he had never before witnessed an allergic reaction such as Kevin's. His face was swollen to four times its normal size, which had restricted his airway. The coroner also noted the extraordinary level of pain killers that were in Kevin's system. He told Mr. Mooney, "What with the high levels of opiates, marijuana, cocaine, and alcohol in his system, I have no idea what it was that finally killed him."

Donny, Joey and Mark met with similar fates, which added to the mystery faced by the Baltimore City coroner. All three boys had suffered some sort of allergic reaction. Donny and

Joey's blood, however, was not laced with large amounts of pain killers, as was Kevin Mooney's. So, they were able to make it back to their beds for the night before the swelling set in. They laid down beneath their sheets in pools of sweat, unable to cry for help as they choked to death. However, in true warrior fashion, Mark Warner fought the longest before succumbing to whatever killed him. When his headaches became unbearable, he managed to make it to St Agnes. In a corner of the ER he writhed and convulsed until his muscles no longer worked. And as his body released more and more histamines to try and fight off the strange allergen that pulsed through his veins, his brain swelled and pressed against his skull until his eyes almost popped out of their sockets.

After he died, police searched Mark's row-home and found conclusive evidence of a dog-fighting ring in his basement, including rows of dog collars hanging like trophies from the pipes in the basement ceiling. Most of the addresses on the collars were from the Violetville and Morrell Park area. Officer Wayne was part of the search team, and my stomach sank when he showed up at my door with his hat in his hands. He had found Ginger's collar in Mark's basement. He told me how much he and his little girl loved to play with Ginger whenever we took walks to his side of Violetville, and that he was sorry about my loss.

I told him, "I'm sure I'll find a way to get over it." It was no consolation, but the deaths of the hoodlums was a good start.

Officer Wayne gave me a wary glance and closed his note pad. His next stop was the other end of the row. They stood outside his house for a while before Mr. Mun went inside and returned with another jar of honey. Officer Wayne grabbed Mr. Mun by the shoulder, and from my stoop I could hear him say, "It's going to be fine, Mun." He looked down at the jar in his hands, smiled and shook it in Mr. Mun's direction, and said as he hustled back to his cruiser, "My prostate thanks you."

•

Life on Pine Heights, post Mark Warner and his gang,

settled back into Violetville's normal, harmonious balance. No

one reported any missing dogs. Ms. Dinkels continued to scare

unwary school children. Mr. Mun had his crew of carpenters

were done fixing his windows in a single day. He also had them

fix the Jonstons' window. My dad continued to know more

about Violetville than any one person should. And everyone

got their honey.

No one missed Kevin Mooney, or even mentioned that he,

Mark, Donny, or Joey ever existed. Mr. Mooney never so much

as looked up towards Mr. Mun's house, and was never again to

receive a jar of honey. In fact, not long after his son died, Mr.

Mooney also passed on. One night he suffered an extreme bout

of sleep apnea and died in a similar fashion as his son.

None of my neighbors cared as much as I did to read the

coroner's reports on the deaths of Mark and his gang. In

memory of Ginger I found them to be satisfactory reading material, and I felt that Violetville was now better off. I also found the reports interesting in that each one claimed that all four boys died as a result of allergic reactions. However, they were unable to determine what was the source of the allergens. The only oddity that they found was a small bug bite or pin prick on each of the victims' backs.